A

NOT

IITIAN

WHY NOT IIT ???

PANTHPREET

SINGH

DEDICATION

This book is dedicated to my mom for believing in me and encouraging me to follow my dreams.

A NOT IITIAN

BACKGROUND:- Once upon a time in Punjab, a woman named Gurleen met a man named Surjeet Singh at a wedding, and they both felt an instant mutual attraction. However, they were both too shy to confess their feelings. After the wedding, they went their separate ways. The next day, Surjeet's sister, Amanat, asked him to accompany them to meet a girl for a potential marriage proposal. Surjeet then confessed to Amanat about Gurleen, and she encouraged him to come along and meet the girl before making any decisions. When they arrived at the girl's house, Surjeet was surprised to see that the girl was none other than Gurleen herself. It was a pure coincidence. Despite this, they agreed to the marriage and got married two months later.

Within a year of their marriage, they had a daughter named Jaspreet, and then two years later, they had another daughter named Namanpreet. They were both pleased and decided not to have any more children. Gurleen then had a copper T procedure, but Surjeet's family was unhappy with their decision as they wanted a son.

They began to mistreat Gurleen by imposing unreasonable restrictions on her, such as forbidding her to cook for her daughters, preventing her from closing the gate while bathing, and even prohibiting her from turning on the fan while sleeping. Surjeet, who served in the Indian army and was frequently away, returned home for a holiday. When Gurleen confided in him about his family's treatment, he reacted by slapping her and accusing her of lying. Although he generally wasn't a bad person, he couldn't bear to hear anything negative about his family. He later apologized to Gurleen for his behavior.

 Gurleen realized that her husband had been manipulated and was unwilling to believe her. Despite her concerns, she remained silent for six years of marriage. Tragically, when Surjeet passed away, her family wrongly blamed Gurleen for his death. This led to a harrowing plot by Amanat and her family to kill Gurleen Kaur and her daughters. Fortunately, a member of the family discovered that Gurleen was six months pregnant at the time, despite having a Copper T. This person secretly informed Gurleen about the plan and helped her escape. With nowhere else to turn, Gurleen fled to Bikaner, where she and Surjeet had planned to purchase a home. Out of fear, she kept her family in the dark about her whereabouts. Despite being highly educated, Gurleen managed to secure a government job at her late husband's workplace. Three months later, she gave birth to a boy and named him PANTHPREET SINGH

<u>CHAPTER 1.</u> A LIFE LESSON - The Undeniable Power Of Wealth

Panthpreet, at the age of 3, was eager to embark on his educational journey as he prepared to join school. He began his academic journey in the town of Lunkaransar, located in the state of Rajasthan, where he completed his 1st and 2nd standards. Although the school he attended was not widely recognized, it provided him with a solid foundation. He continued his studies and completed his education up to the 12th grade in Bikaner, where he further honed his academic skills.

The school that Panth enrolled in during the 3rd standard was a prestigious institution in the city known for its strong emphasis on English language education. Unlike his peers, who were already well-versed in English, Panth had not been exposed to the language previously, which made him feel somewhat out of place among his classmates. Recognizing his hesitation, his class teacher, Mrs. Anamika, took an interest in helping him. She kindly invited him to join her for lunch, during which she handed him a book and requested that he read the first page. Despite struggling with his pronunciation, Panth put forth his best effort, and Mrs. Anamika took notice of his determination and eagerness to learn the language.

She advised Panth that to truly grasp the English language, he should commit to speaking only in English for the entirety of the following week. Without hesitation, Panth vowed to adhere to her advice and followed through. Despite facing ridicule from some students, he remained resolute in his commitment to speaking only English. Mrs. Anamika recognized his dedication and observed his growing confidence. The next day, his teacher summoned him to the front of the class and lauded his unwavering efforts. Encouraged by this praise, Panth blossomed into a fluent and self-assured English speaker, forging new friendships along the way. Despite joining the school midterm with a backlog of syllabi, his hard work paid off as he emerged as the top performer in his class.

As Panth's interest in acquiring new skills grew, his passion for sports, including Cricket, Football, and Kabaddi, became apparent. He consistently excelled in various areas, demonstrating outstanding performance in academics, sports, annual dramas, dance performances, and more.

He was incredibly caring towards his mother and sisters, as they were his only family. One day, he came across a news story about a girl who had been horrifically assaulted, then set on fire and discarded. Although he was still very young and didn't fully comprehend the situation, the disturbing images made him realize that the girl had suffered immensely. He turned to his teacher for an explanation of what had happened.

The teacher imparted valuable wisdom about the principles of good and bad deeds. Furthermore, the teacher emphasized that to safeguard and serve the community, it would be essential for him to pursue a career in civil services.

In the 4th grade, Panth experienced an emotional moment when his beloved teacher, Mrs. Anamika, left the school. However, in both the 4th and 5th grades, he was fortunate to have Mrs. Beenu as his class teacher.

Mrs. Beenu held a special fondness for Panth, seeing him not just as a student, but also as a remarkable child. She instilled in him the values of hard work, patience, and perseverance. Though she was a strict teacher, Panth held a deep admiration for the principles she upheld, which included punctuality, her dignified personality, and her sense of style.

In the 5th grade, he eagerly decided to join a local cricket academy to pursue his passion for the sport. His commitment and dedication led him to Jaipur for the under-14 trials in the 6th grade, accompanied by his coach and fellow players. The excitement and tension were palpable as he stepped into the nets for the trials. After the trials, the invigilator was quick to commend his performance, which filled him with a sense of pride and accomplishment. Meanwhile, his friend Abhishek, who had also participated in the trials, faced a challenging time, being bowled out four times in just 12 balls. Despite this, his friend remained surprisingly cheerful, leaving the protagonist curious about the reasons behind Abhishek's unwavering happiness, even after a tough performance.

In the tranquil evening, as the participants gathered together, anxiously awaiting the results, Panth was taken aback when Abhishek's name was called as the selected candidate, while his name was not. Confusion marred his face, even as his coach approached the team to confirm the results. Seeking answers, Panth turned to Abhishek and learned that the selector was a close friend of his father's and that he had paid a significant sum of 20 thousand rupees for each round he played. In that moment, Panth's eyes were opened to the harsh reality of society: the undeniable power of wealth.

<u>CHAPTER 2.</u> **CORONAVIRUS** - **The Quarantine**

As Panth completed his trials and arrived in Bikaner, the world was struck by a devastating new threat - the coronavirus. Panth and his mother, both battling asthma, now faced an even deadlier challenge as the virus wreaked havoc on patients with respiratory conditions. The response was swift as the entire nation and then the world went into lockdown. Once bustling streets lay empty, devoid of children playing in schools or parks, and devoid of the usual office activity. This period marked one of the most unprecedented and challenging times the world had ever seen.

Panth's heart was filled with dread, not for his safety, but for that of his mother. His worst fears materialized when his mother received a positive test result for the virus. The news came with a directive for a midnight transfer to the hospital. Faced with the prospect of leaving her young children, she pleaded with the medical team to allow her to quarantine at home. Recognizing the predicament, the compassionate team captain granted her request for home quarantine.

After a couple of days, four of them tested positive for the virus and were brought to Vijay Verghiya Dhani, A prestigious hotel on the outskirts of Bikaner., for quarantine. Panth developed serious symptoms and was struggling to breathe. He was afraid of dying but eventually received treatment. Soon, they made friends at the quarantine and enjoyed their time.

THE QUARANTINE - In the early mornings, they would all rise promptly and convene on the grounds for a hearty breakfast. Following this, an array of games such as Kho-Kho, football, ludo, and truth or dare would commence. Panth had a particular penchant for video games, and would often engage in sessions of Free Fire and PUBG. The camaraderie and enjoyment they experienced during these activities made their time together truly memorable.

Every evening, they underwent testing, and only those who received negative results were permitted to return home. After a month of being in quarantine, all four individuals tested negative and were finally able to return home. The quarantine period had a profound impact on their lives, leaving behind both negative and positive memories. These included the bonds of friendship they formed, terrifying experiences they encountered, the fear of losing someone, and the very real fear of death. Eventually, as the world became free from the virus, life began to return to normal gradually.

As Panth bid farewell to his best friend from school, Mayank, who was leaving for Australia to pursue further studies, he felt a heavy weight of emotions settling in. They used to spend entire days together, and Mayank had even been a frequent guest at Panth's house. The impending separation left Panth feeling nostalgic and melancholic. It was during this time of emotional upheaval that he met a girl named Aditi.

CHAPTER 3. THE FRIENDSHIP - Life Goes On.

Aditi, the new girl who had recently joined their school, was assigned as his bench partner. As they prepared for an inter-school competition together, diligently working as a team, their bond deepened, and a strong friendship began to blossom. They quickly swapped phone numbers and found themselves deep in conversation for hours each day. Their classmates couldn't help but notice their growing bond. Aditi, with her striking looks, intelligence, and self-assurance, attracted the attention of many boys, but she only opened up to Panth and found it difficult to connect with others. A similar situation applied to Panth: he was good-looking, intelligent, and excelled in sports, which made him popular, but he was not very comfortable around others.

Panth and Aditi found themselves in 10th grade. Panth was unwavering in his pursuit of a career in civil services, while he couldn't help but notice that Aditi seemed to be somewhat nonchalant about her aspiration to become a scientist. Sensing something amiss, Panth confronted Aditi, and it was then that she confessed her burgeoning romantic feelings for him. However, Panth only sees Aditi as his best friend and nothing else. When Panth expressed his feelings, Aditi didn't reciprocate, leading to the unfortunate loss of Panth's second best friend. As they embarked on their higher studies, they parted ways, and their farewell marked the end of their communication.

Panth decided to pursue his undergraduate studies at IIT, which led him to relocate to Kota, a city in Rajasthan, for his 11th and 12th-grade education as well as preparations for the IIT entrance exams. He chose to join a relatively lesser-known coaching institute to aid him in his preparations. However, during his 11th grade, he encountered challenges when one of his teachers consistently missed classes, resulting in only half of the syllabus being covered by the end of the year. Consequently, Panth opted to seek out a new institution with a strong reputation and widespread recognition to continue his studies.

On the first day of coaching, Panth attended his favorite subject, Mathematics. He was in awe of the teacher's ability to explain complex topics in a way that was easy to understand. This newfound clarity and understanding motivated Panth to double his efforts and approach the upcoming exam with confidence. Six months before the exams, as Panth was on his way hostel one evening, he caught sight of a girl. It was dark, and she was wearing a helmet, so he couldn't make out her outfit. However, her eyes were piercing and left a lasting impression on him. Panth paused, watching as the girl walked away, leaving him spellbound by the divine beauty of her eyes. In that moment, for the first time, Panth experienced the overwhelming emotions of love.

The next day, a new girl, who turned out to be the same girl he had seen the night before, joined Panth's coaching class. He was surprised and thought it was the best thing to happen to him. Though he wanted to talk to her, he was too shy. As days passed, he found himself unable to utter a word, yet he couldn't help but steal glances at her throughout every session. On the day of a test, students had to fill out their attendance sheets, providing their names and mobile numbers. Panth saw this as an opportunity to obtain her name and number. He hurried to fill the sheet just after her, pushing through many students and managed to learn her mobile number and her name TINA.

TINA -Panth, upon returning to his hostel, found himself contemplating a reason to text her. He decided to ask for the notes from today's session, despite already possessing them. Despite his efforts to sleep, he found himself awake all night, eagerly anticipating her response. The following Sunday afternoon, he received a reply asking, "Excuse me, who are you?" Panth felt disappointed in himself for neglecting to include his name in the initial text. Consequently, he disclosed his name to her and clarified that he was her batchmate. After sending the notes, Panth felt an overwhelming sense of shame for lying. Despite his prior belief that expressing interest directly was acceptable, he admitted to having the notes and expressed a desire to engage in conversation. He went on to confess that he had never been a believer in love, particularly the idea of love at first sight. However, upon encountering her, he found himself deeply captivated, and she was the one who inspired him to reconsider his beliefs. From the moment he laid eyes on her, he felt entirely entranced and hoped to establish a genuine friendship with her.

Tina was taken aback by his honesty, but she concealed her surprise behind a facade of anger. She summoned him to meet at a cozy café near the college before the start of classes. Panth, visibly shaken, reluctantly agreed to the meeting. Upon meeting at the café, they both ordered cold coffee. Panth sat in silence, his facial expression betraying his deep-seated fear. Tina reassured him and shared that as a newcomer to the city, she was desperate for a friend, sparking the beginning of their enduring friendship.

As their friendship deepened, they found themselves spending the majority of their time together. They cherished each other's company and grew inseparable. With just 4 months remaining until the exams, they were making good progress in their studies, but Panth felt the need to dedicate more time to his academics. Tina empathized with his concerns, and they decided to limit their meetings to the hostel. There, she assisted him with daily tasks before they settled down to study side by side. While Tina focused on Mathematics and Physics, Panth advised her to also concentrate on Chemistry, emphasizing the importance of having a strong foundation in all three subjects for the JEE ADVANCED exam. Tina attempted to develop an interest in chemistry, but since she couldn't, she continued studying the same way as before.

Both Panth and Tina had consistently excelled in their coaching tests, earning the confidence and praise of their teachers. As the exams loomed just a month away, Panth couldn't help but notice the prolonged stress etched on Tina's face. Concerned, he inquired, and she confided in him about the pressure from her parents. Despite her academic aspirations, they expected her to assume responsibility for her father's thriving business in Mumbai, citing her age of 18 as justification. Her father, a prominent and affluent figure in the Mumbai business world, seemed to have already decided her path.

She was filled with worry at the thought of not passing her exams and the possible consequences of being unable to continue her studies as a result. Panth's reassurance that she would do well somehow managed to ease her anxiety. The following morning, while enjoying a cup of coffee with Tina, Panth was caught off guard as Tina shared her heartfelt feelings with him. Panth was overjoyed beyond words. He couldn't contain his happiness, staying awake the entire night and beaming from ear to ear the next day in class. This feeling was the most euphoric Panth had ever experienced, and they were truly having a good time together.

Their highly anticipated JEE MAINS exams loomed just a week away. With their preparatory classes now closed, they eagerly decided to reunite immediately after their pivotal exams. Coincidentally, they discovered that they were assigned the same date and shift for the exam, yet different examination centers. Before parting ways, they exchanged heartfelt wishes of luck and eagerly headed to take on the challenge. When they reunited the following day, the air was thick with palpable confidence and beaming happiness. With a sense of eager anticipation, they both went online to check their exam papers and were pleased with their performance.

After the results were announced, Panth achieved an outstanding 98.94 percentile with All India Rank 10320, while Tine scored an impressive 97.39 percentile with

AIR 36542. Both of them celebrated their selection for the JEE ADVANCED exam, which was scheduled to take place in three months. Their remarkable scores not only boosted their confidence but also fueled their interest in the upcoming preparations. Despite studying together, Panth constantly encouraged Tine to focus more on her Chemistry studies, but Tine struggled to muster interest in the subject. As time passed, the day of their exam finally arrived. Both when went to the center were worried but confident.

When they met again, Tina appeared disheartened by her performance. She expressed concerns about barely passing Chemistry but remained confident about her performance in Physics and Mathematics. Panth reassured her and advised her not to worry too much. With their exams completed, they both began their journey home.

Nine days after the results were announced, Panth eagerly looked at his score: AIR 8662. He felt a surge of joy and relief. Excited to share the good news with Tina, he tried calling her, but she didn't answer. He suspected her parents were probably restricting her from using her phone. Panth decided to meet her at the coaching center's farewell ceremony, hoping to see her there. Three days later, at the emotional farewell event, to his surprise, Tina was nowhere to be found. Deeply concerned, he approached his teacher and asked about Tina's absence. The teacher's response was shocking and heartbreaking. The teacher explained that Tina's disappointing exam results had led her parents to force her into joining their family business. Overwhelmed by the pressures and her academic struggles, Tina succumbed to her deep despair and took her own life. Panth was shattered by the tragic twist of fate. Panth then made a brave decision that went against the wishes of his family and society.

<u>CHAPTER 4 -</u> **THE DECISION** - A Proof

****** **TO BE CONTINUED** ******

ACKNOWLEDGEMENTS______

To God, for your loving guidance and for the many blessings you have bestowed upon me.

To my mother, Mrs. Harvinder Kaur, for your love and support, and for the code of ethics you taught me, which has served me so well in my life.

To my sisters, Jaspeet Kaur and Namanpreet Kaur, for your enthusiastic support of my work

To my pet Peeco, for always loving me, no matter what.